Who Took That Dog?

BY TRACE TAYLOR

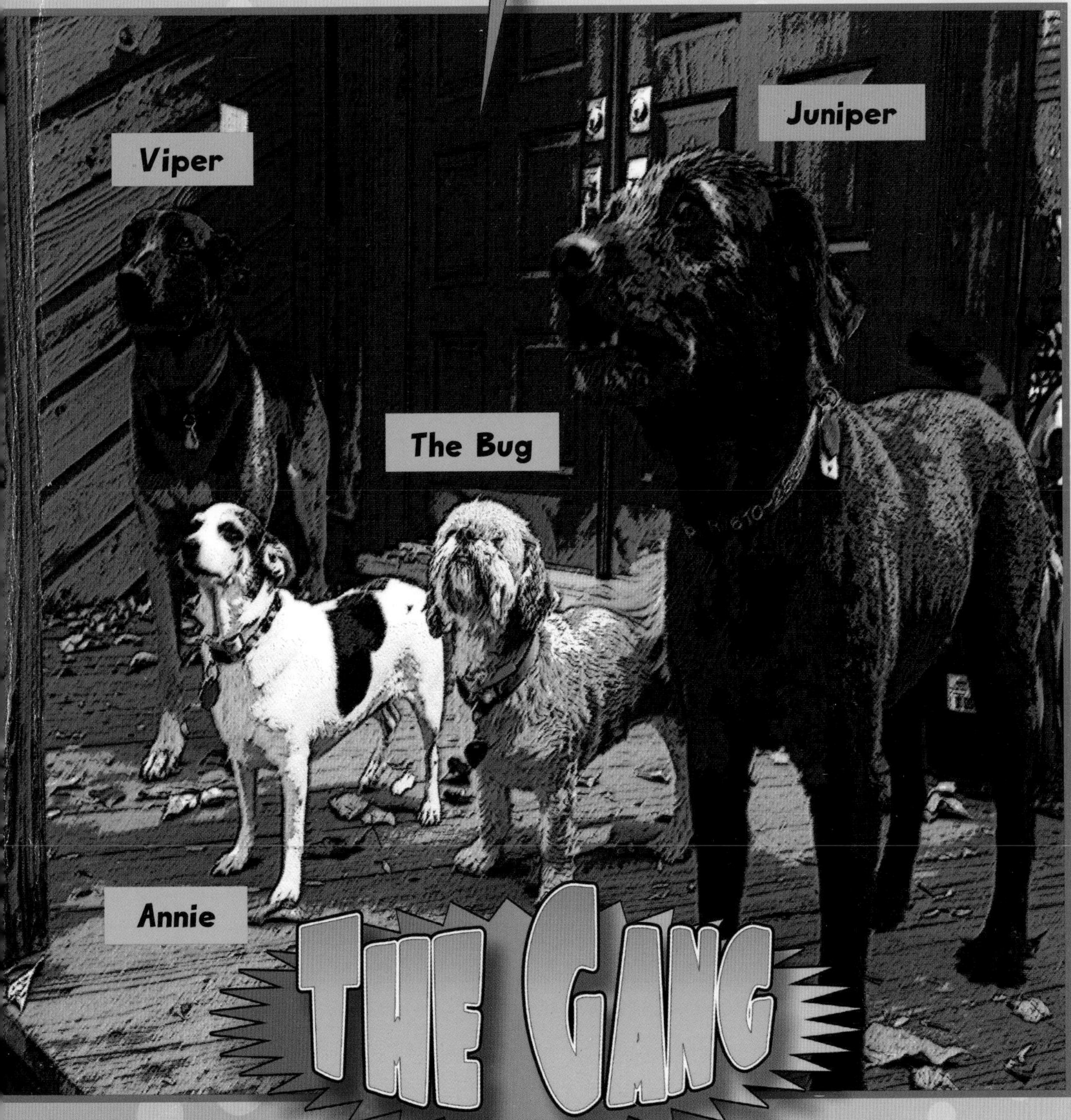
Viper
Juniper
The Bug
Annie
THE GANG

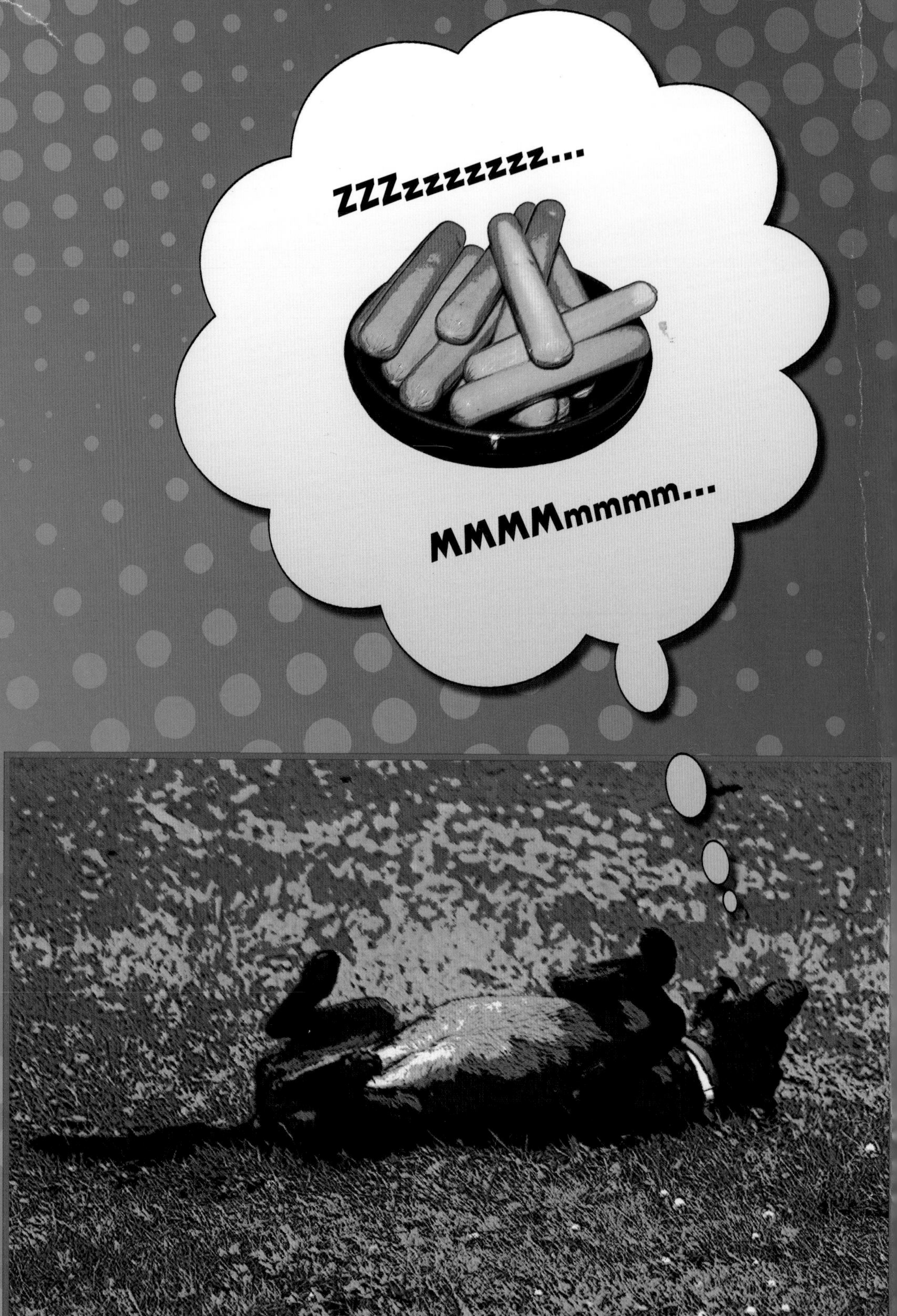
ZZZzzzzzzz...
MMMMmmmmm...

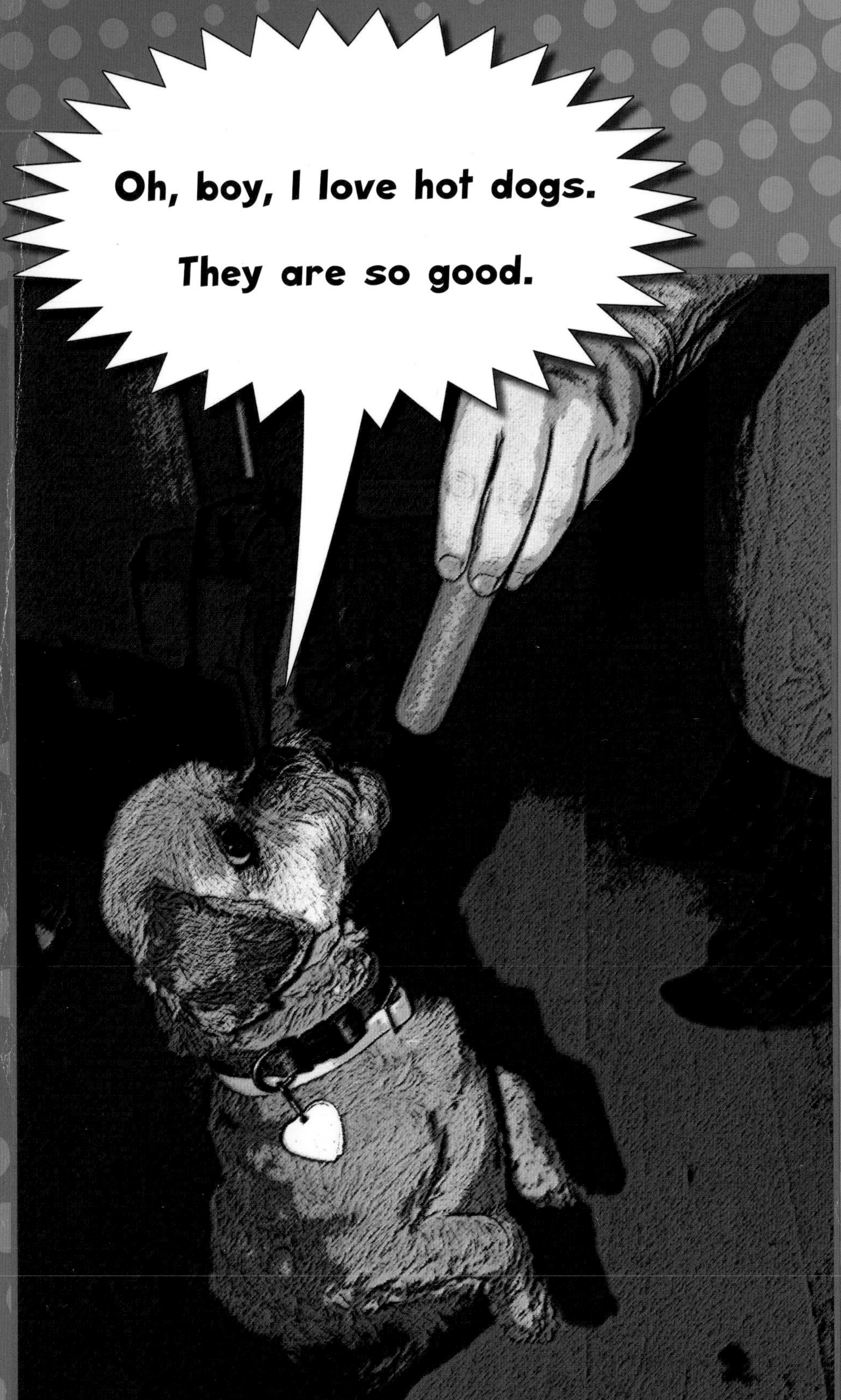
Oh, boy, I love hot dogs.
They are so good.

I'm not going to eat it now.

I'll save it.

I'll hide it in the yard by the tree.

It will be safe there.

No one will find it here.

I will come back for it.

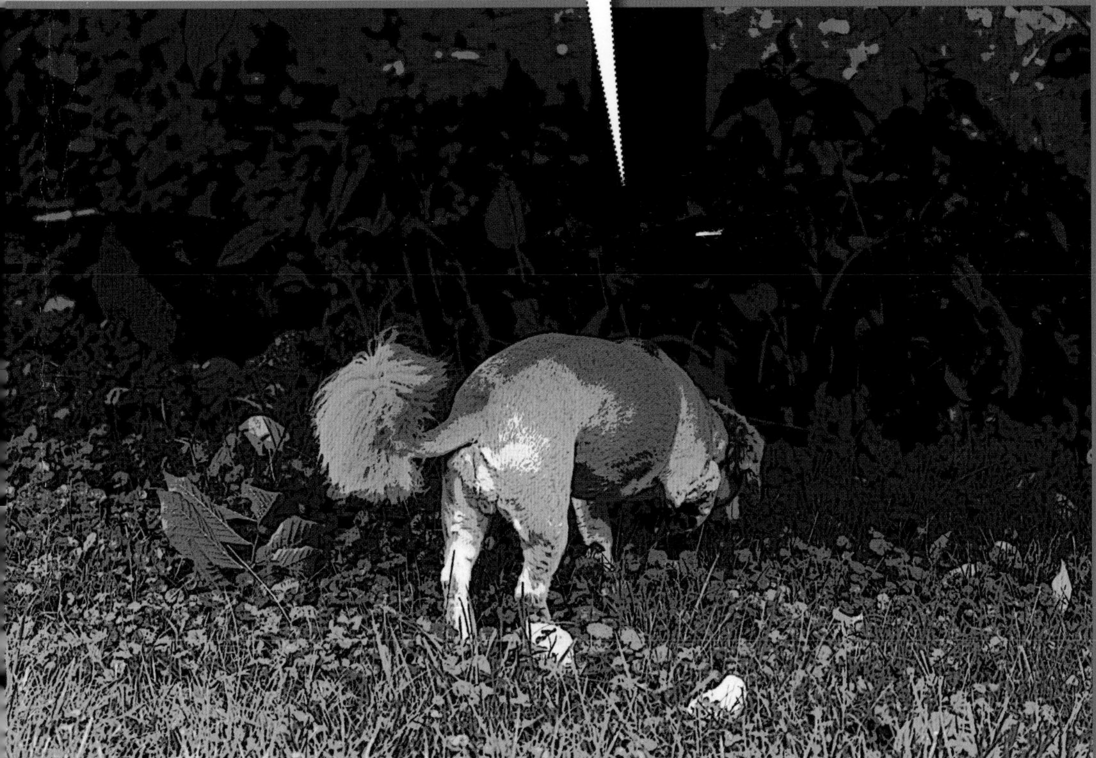

Hot dog?

Did I hear the words "hot dog"?

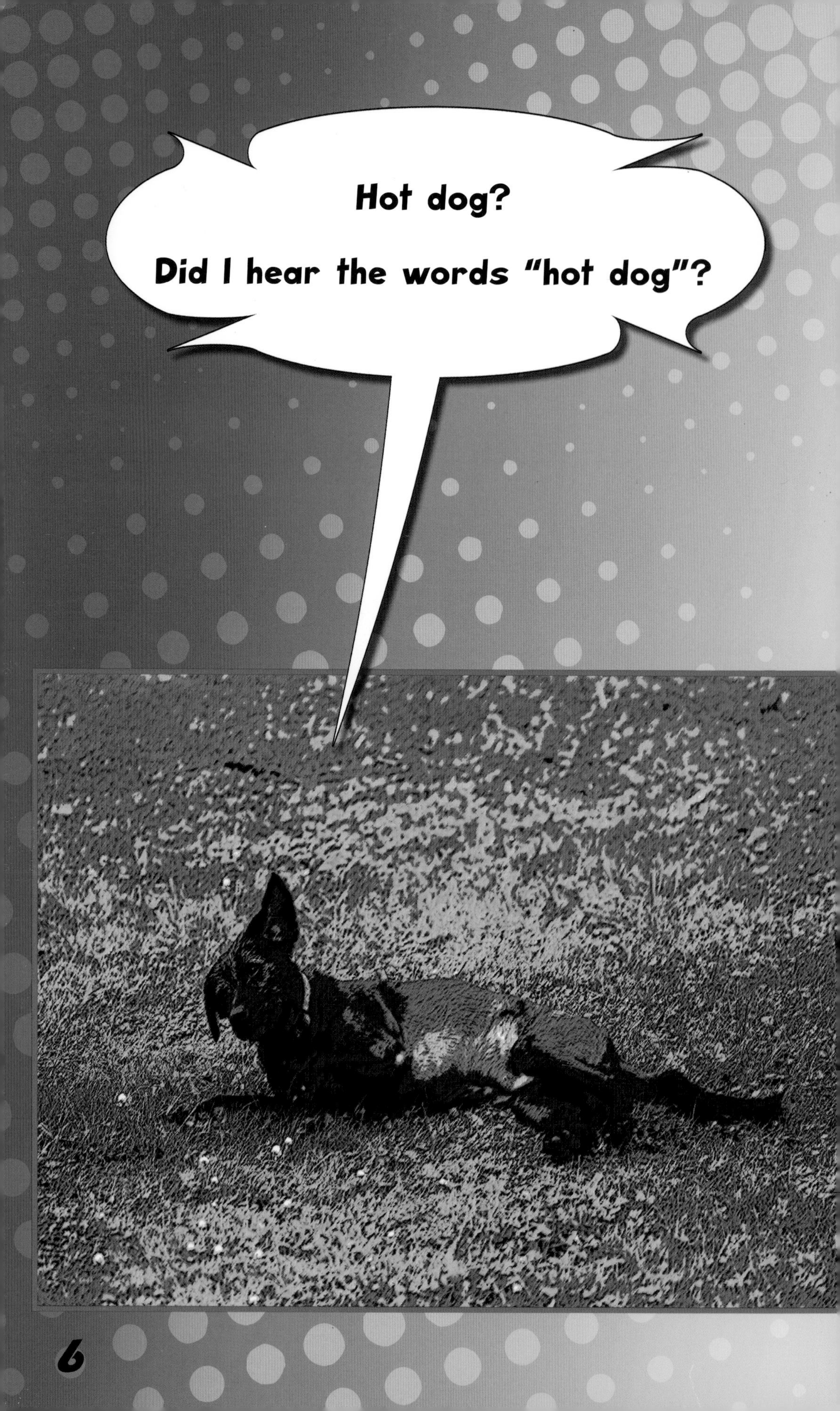

I smell them.

They must be close.

Where are they?

I want them.

I want them all.

There they are, in that hole by the tree.

I love them.

I love them so much.

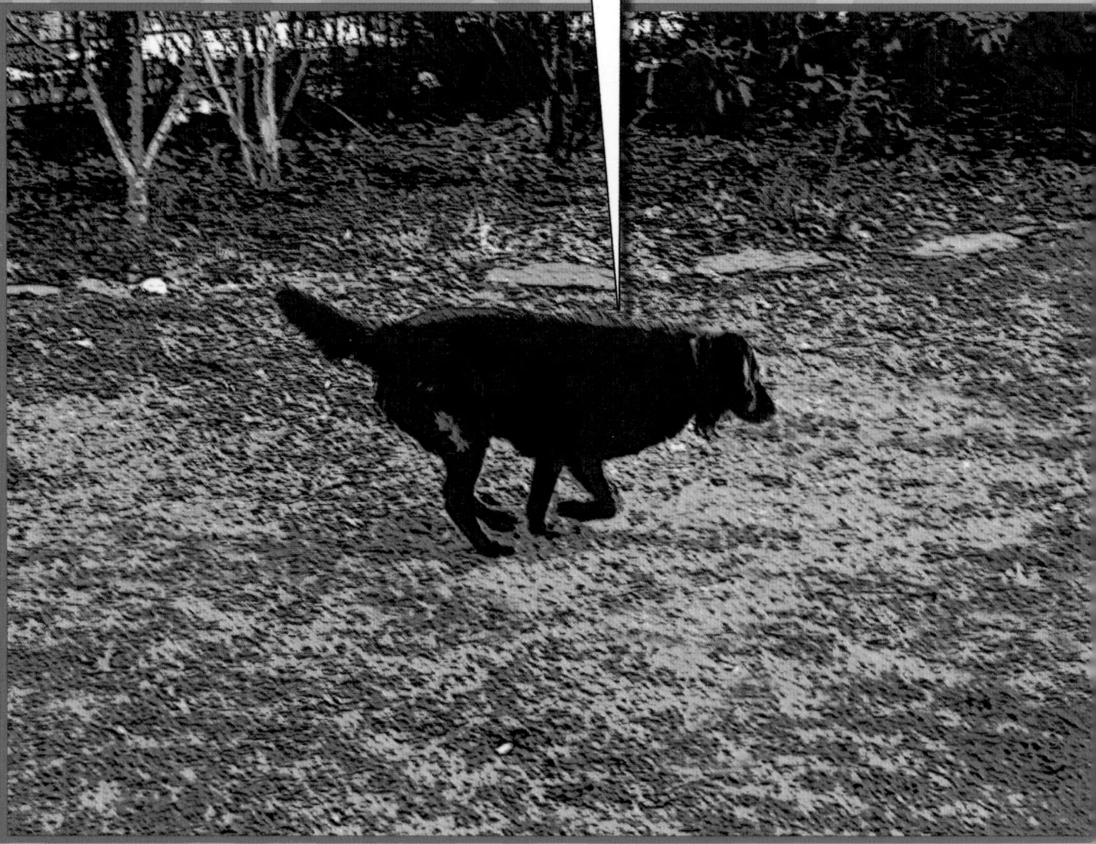

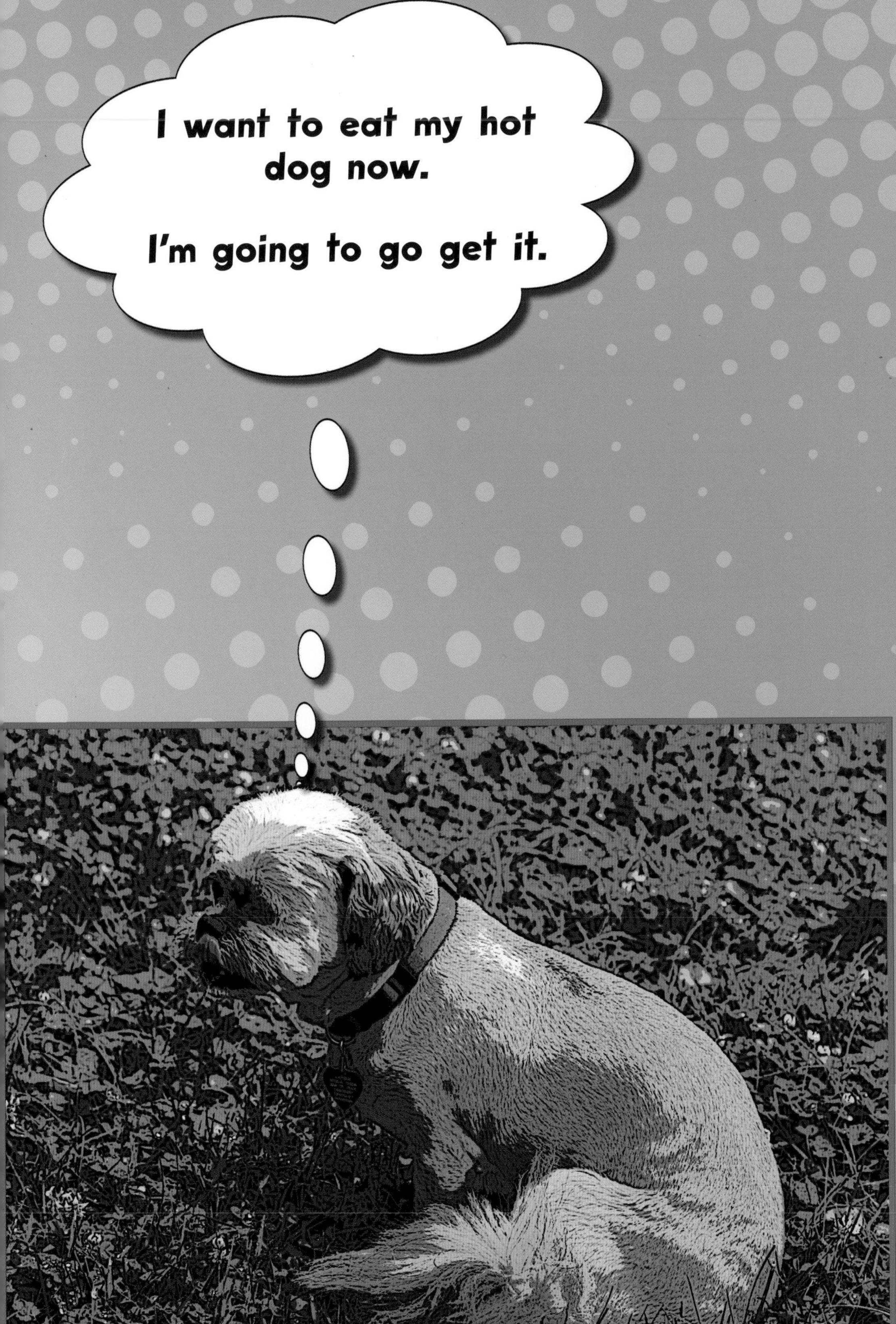
I want to eat my hot dog now.
I'm going to go get it.

This is where I put it,
but it isn't here.

Where did it go?

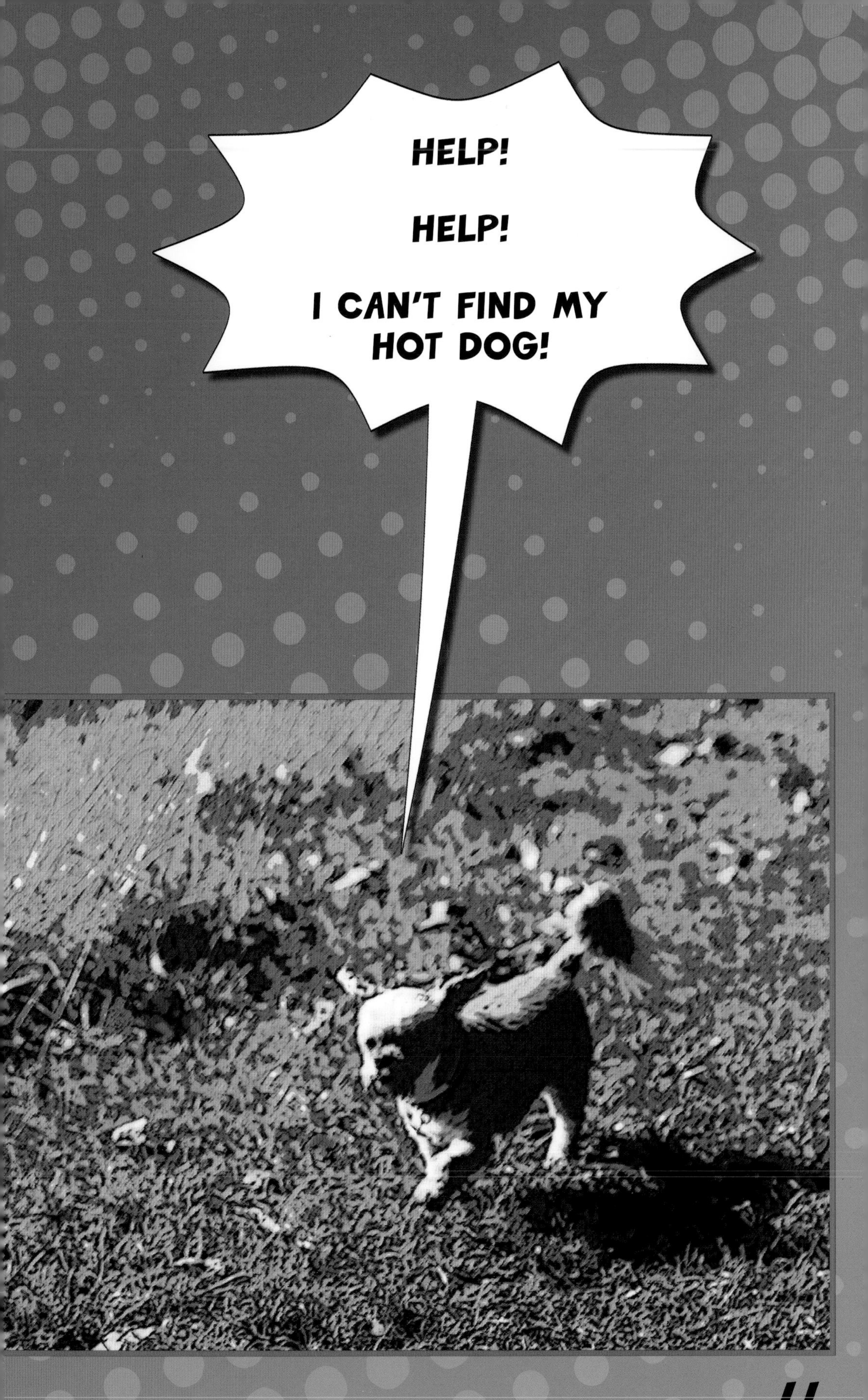
HELP!
HELP!
I CAN'T FIND MY HOT DOG!

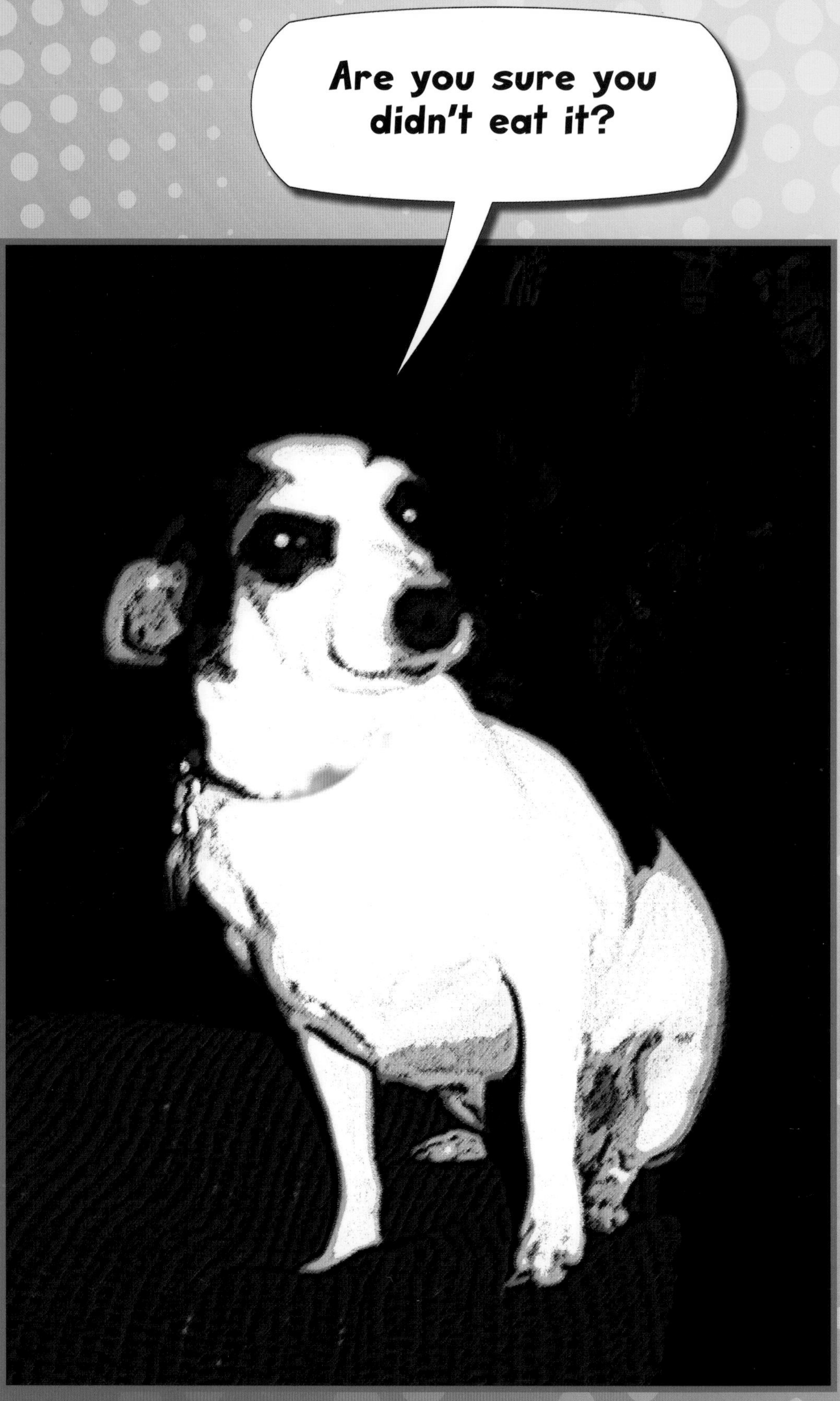
Are you sure you didn't eat it?

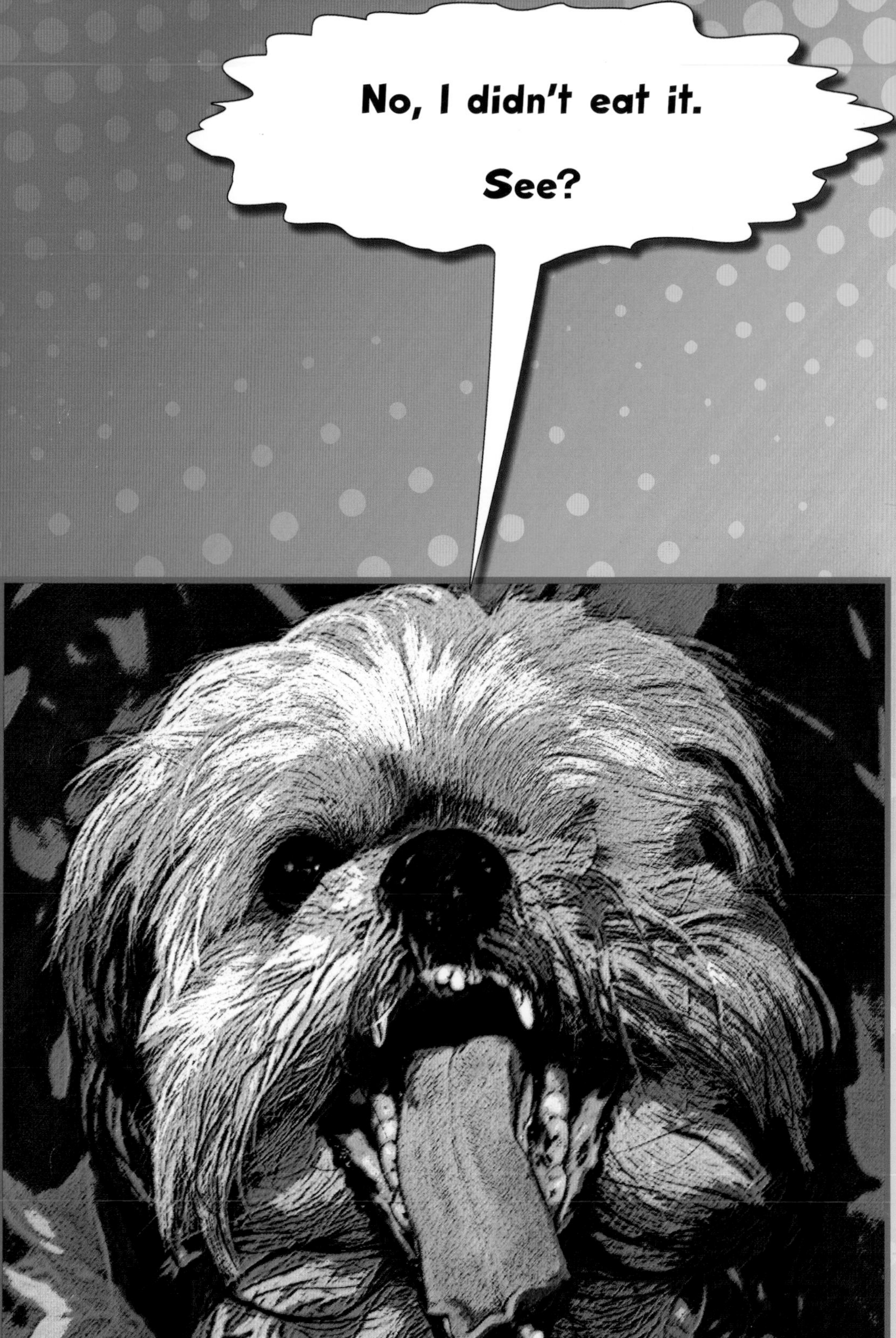
No, I didn't eat it.
See?

Nope, not in there.

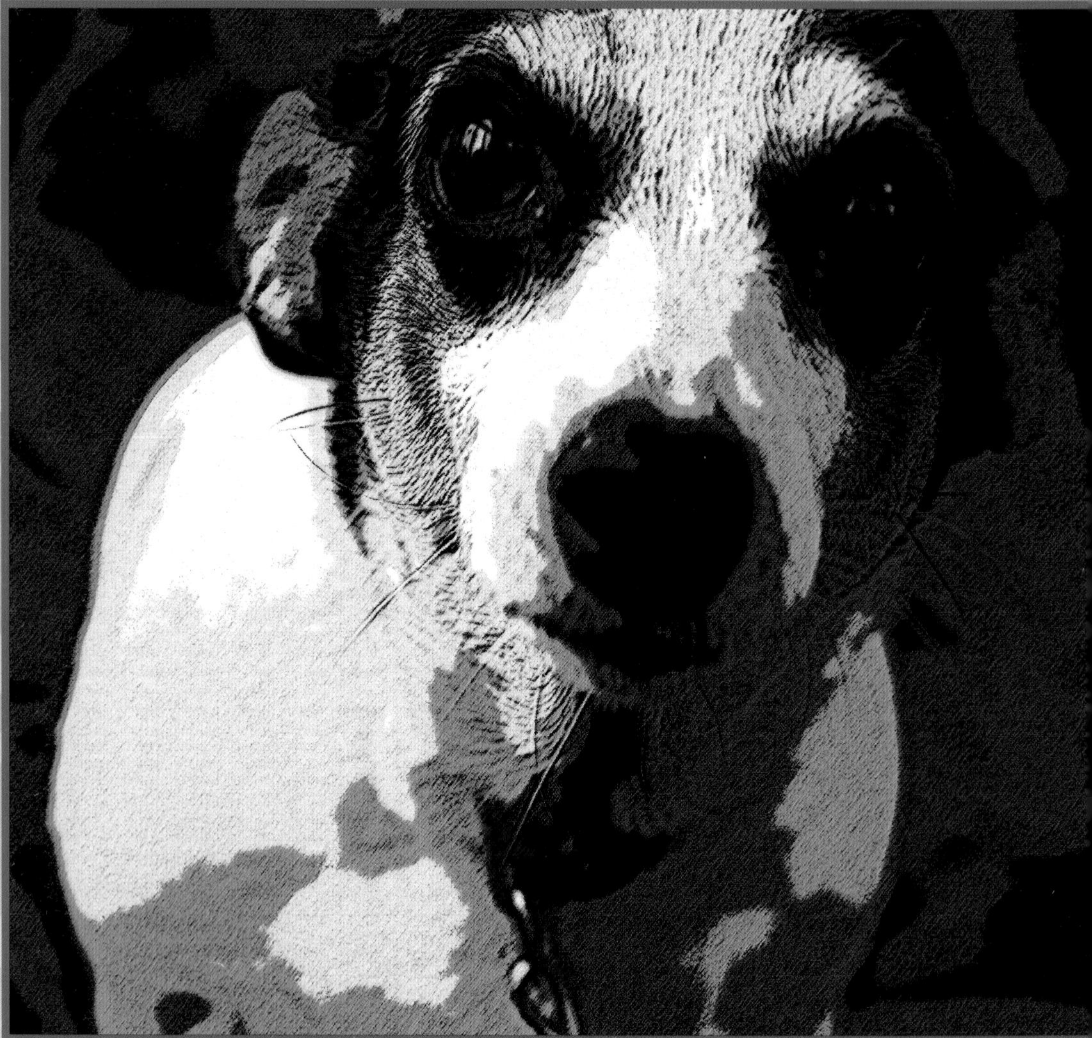

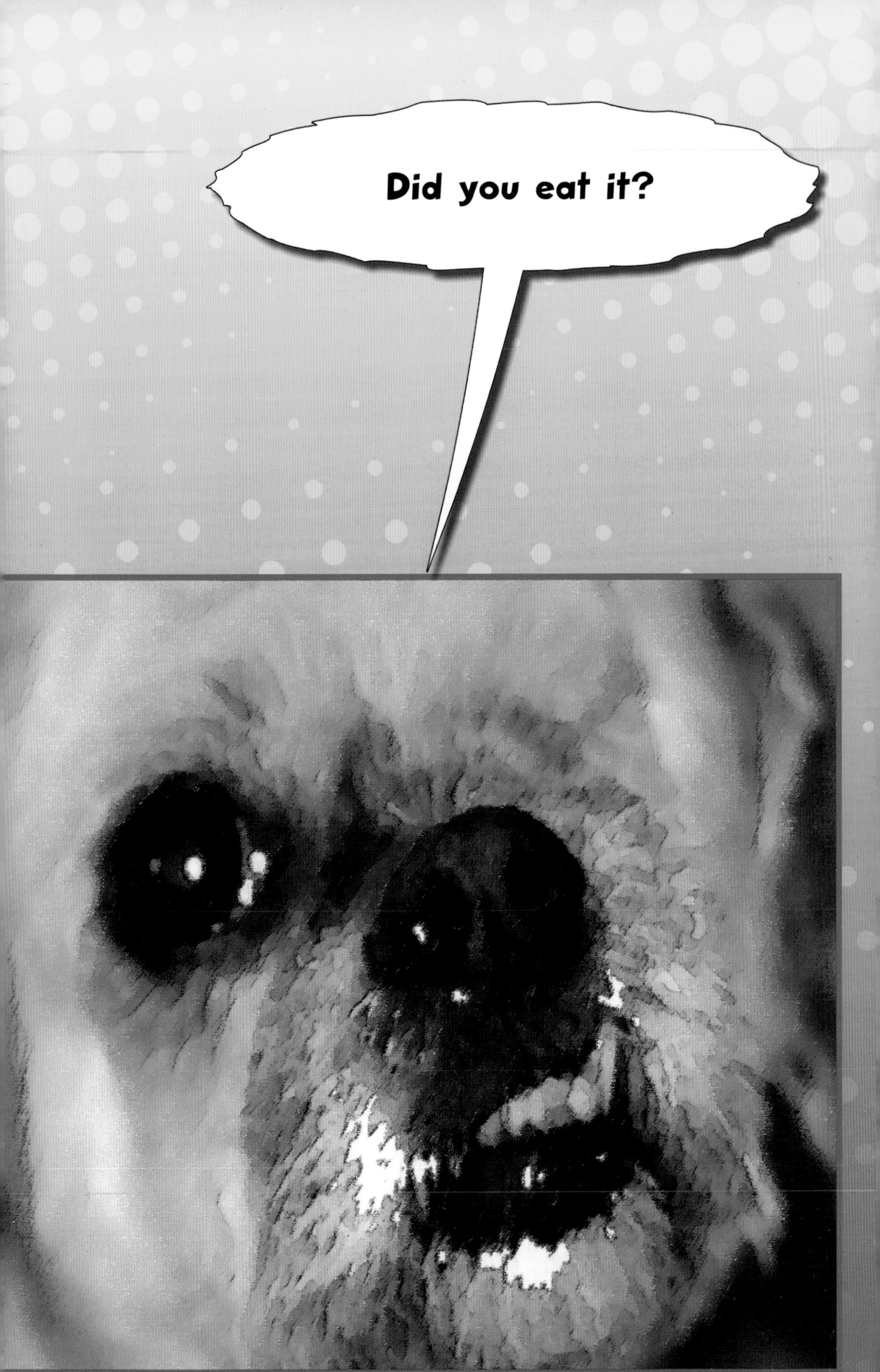
Did you eat it?

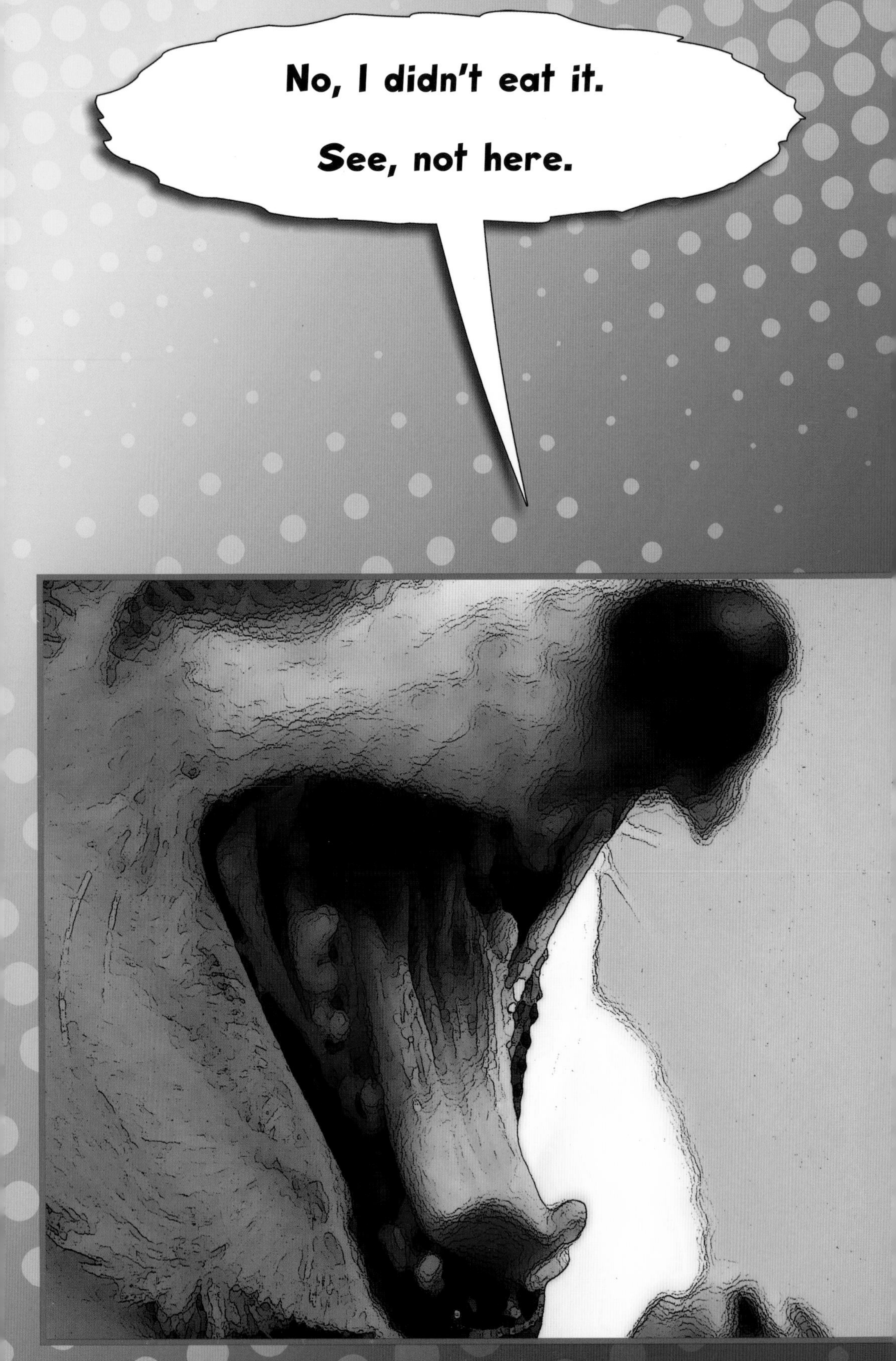
No, I didn't eat it.
See, not here.

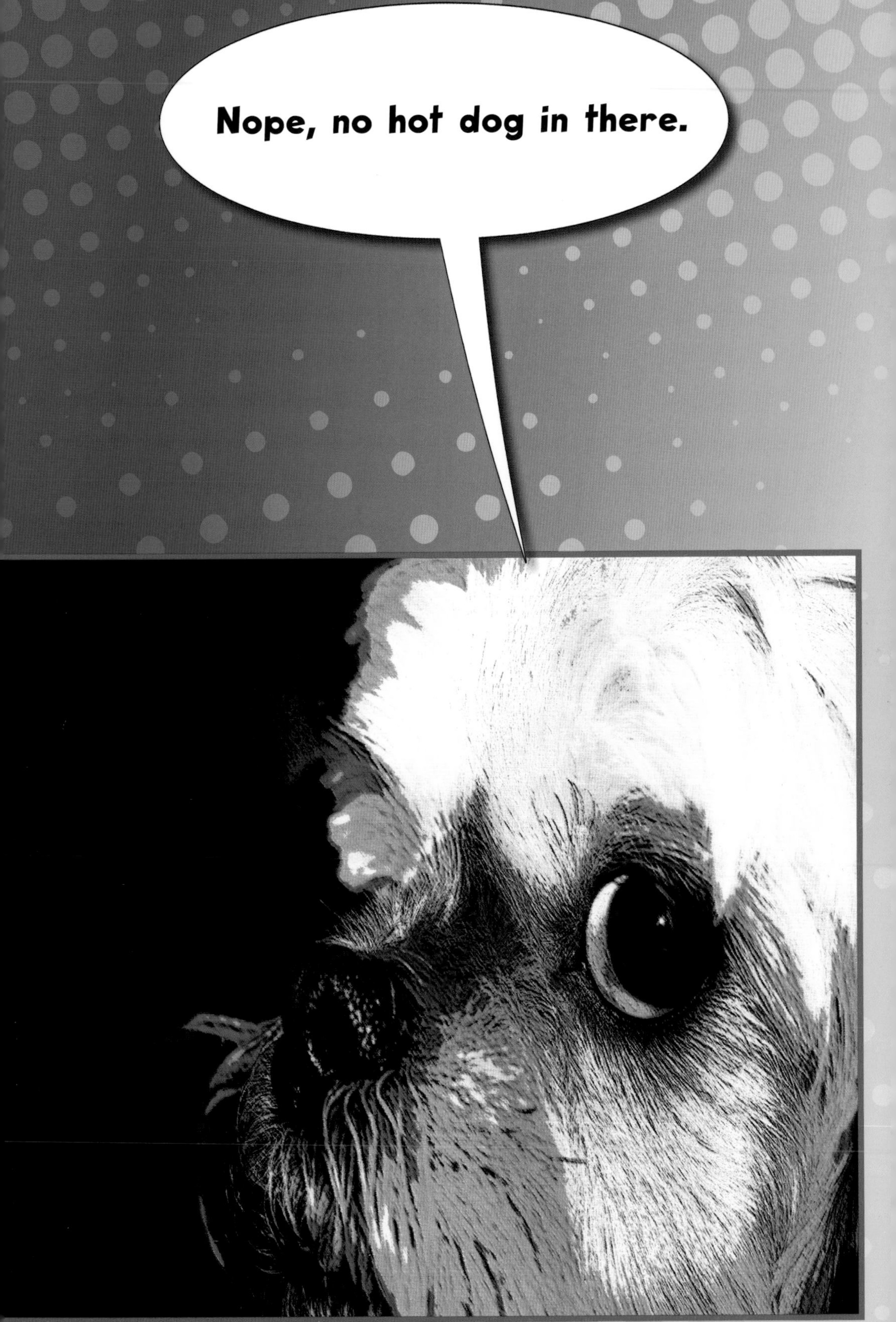
Nope, no hot dog in there.

Have you seen it?

Do you know where it is?

Did you eat it?

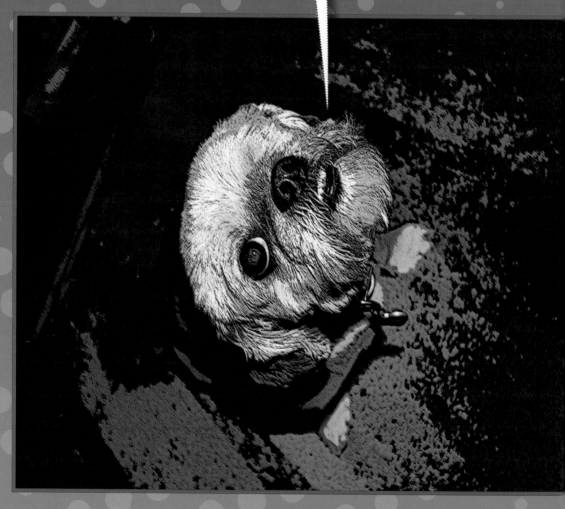

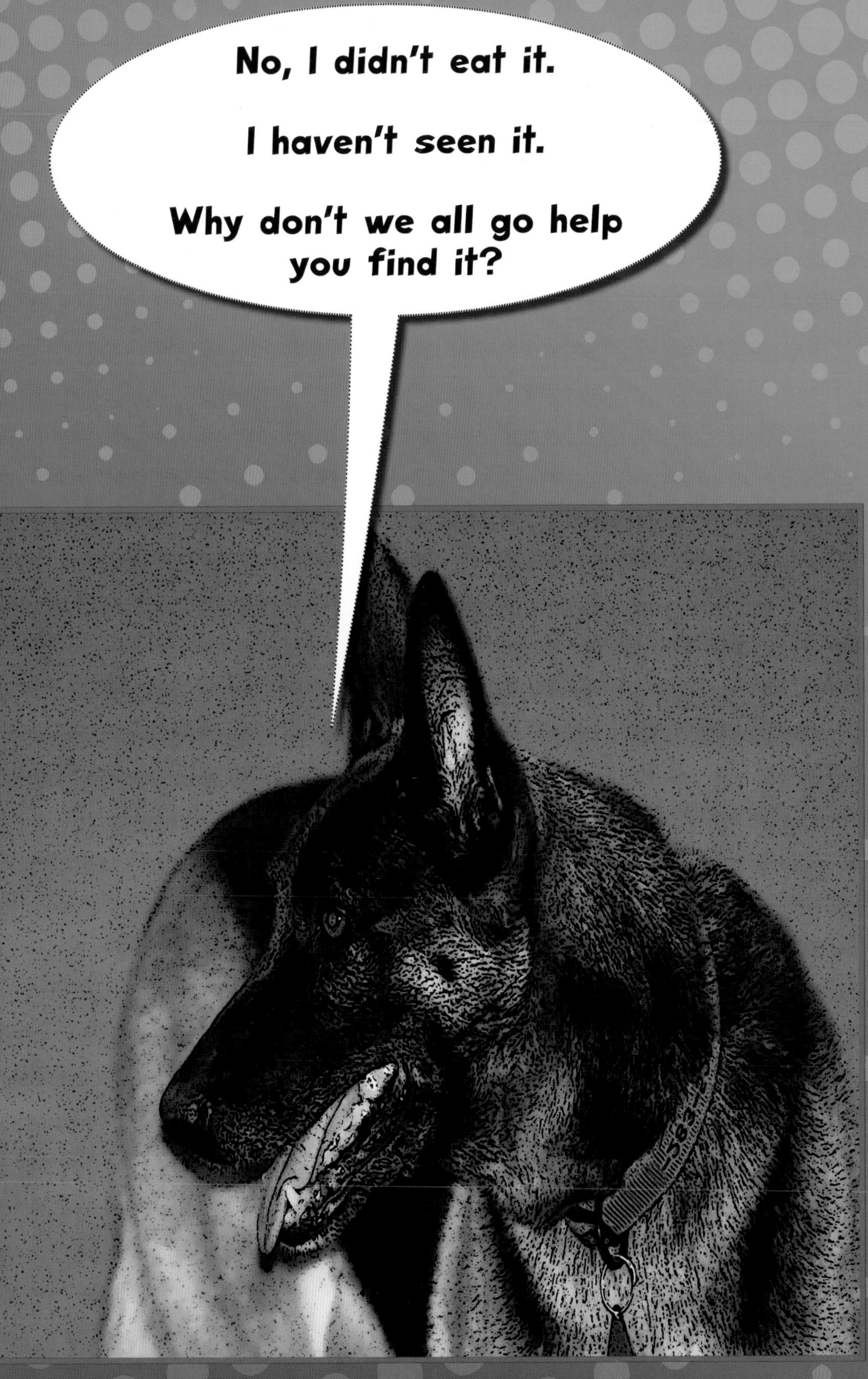
No, I didn't eat it.
I haven't seen it.
Why don't we all go help you find it?

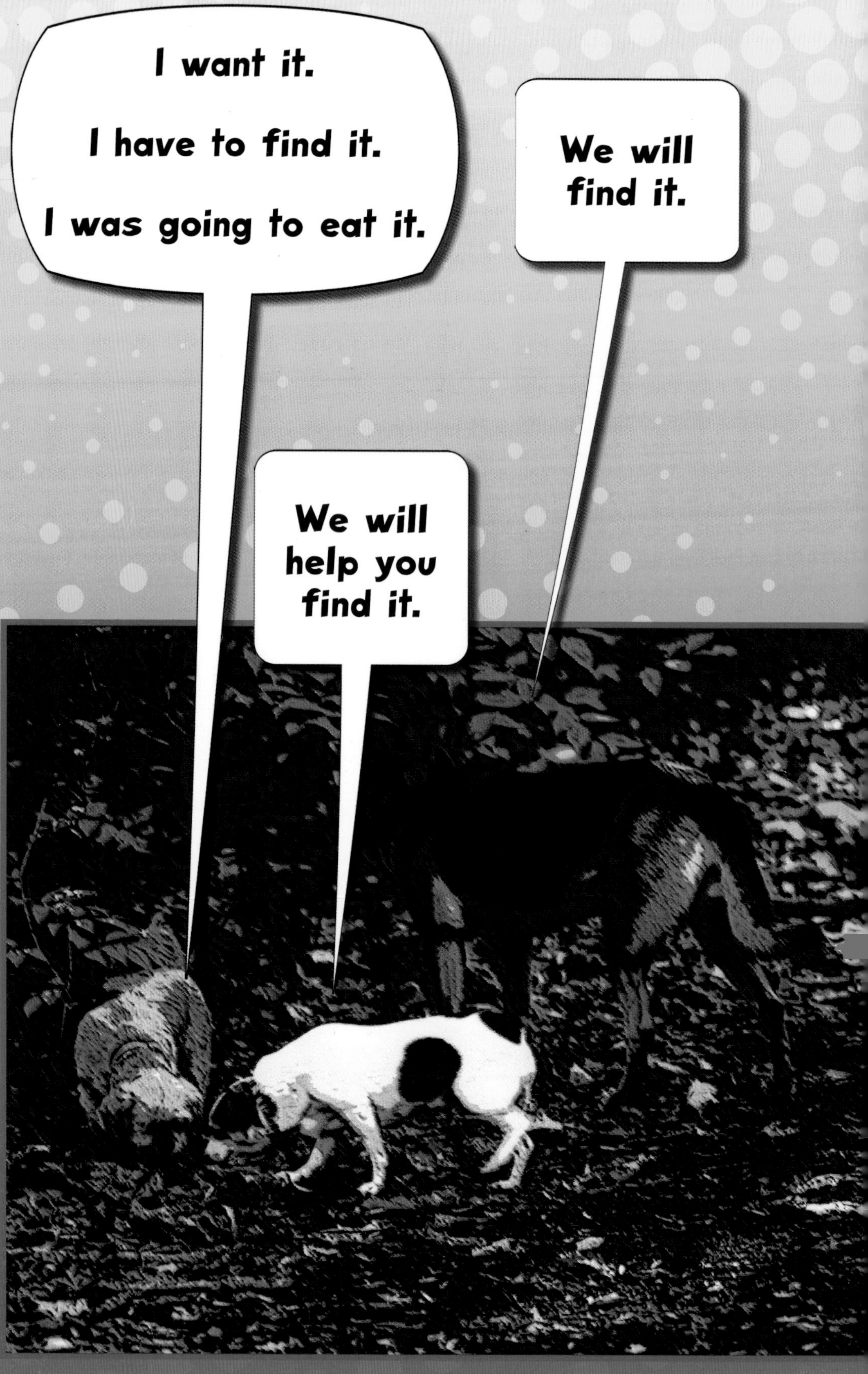
I want it.
I have to find it.
I was going to eat it.
We will find it.
We will help you find it.

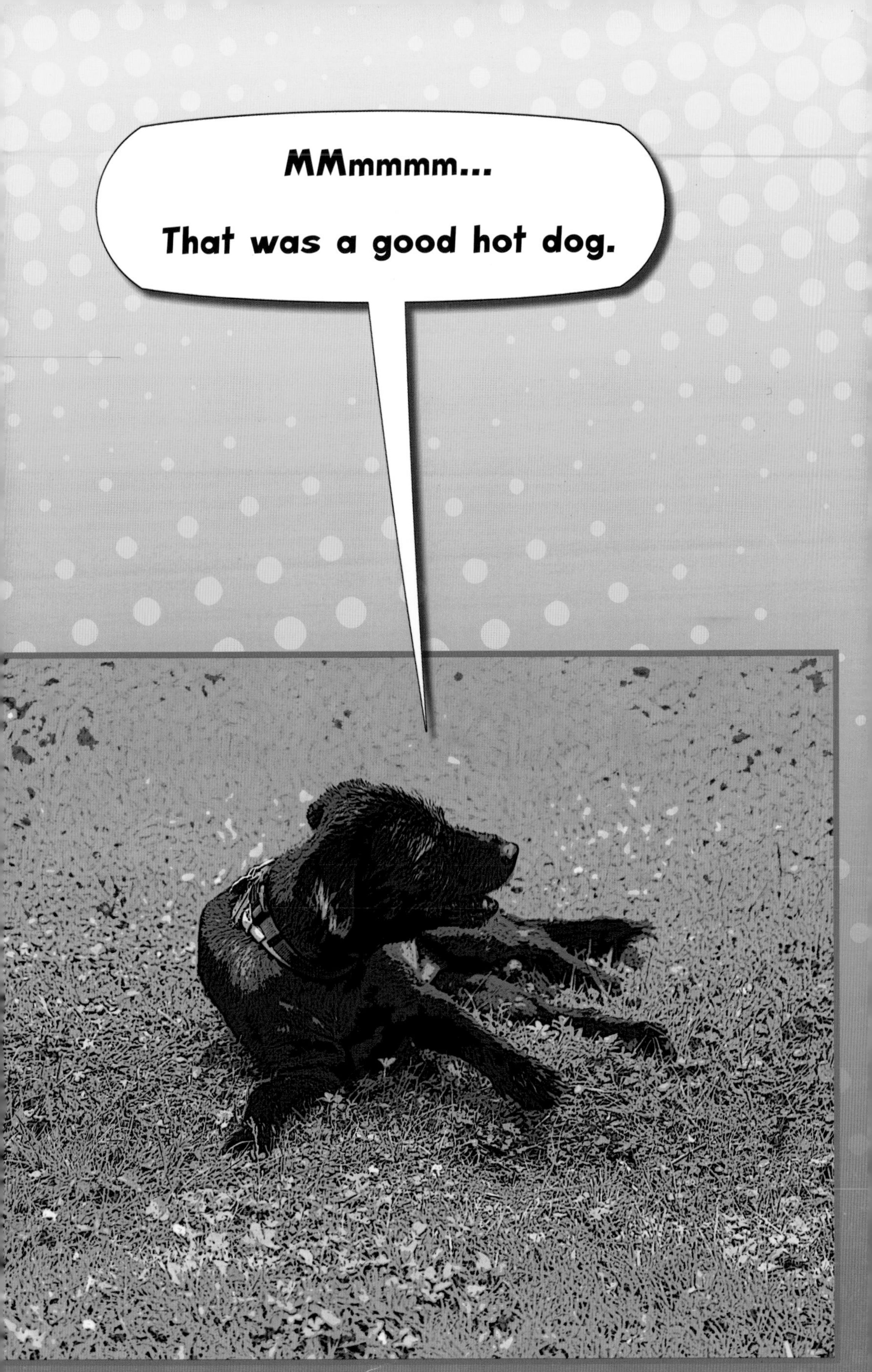
MMmmmm...
That was a good hot dog.

Stop that bad dog!

Get her!

She ate the hot dog.

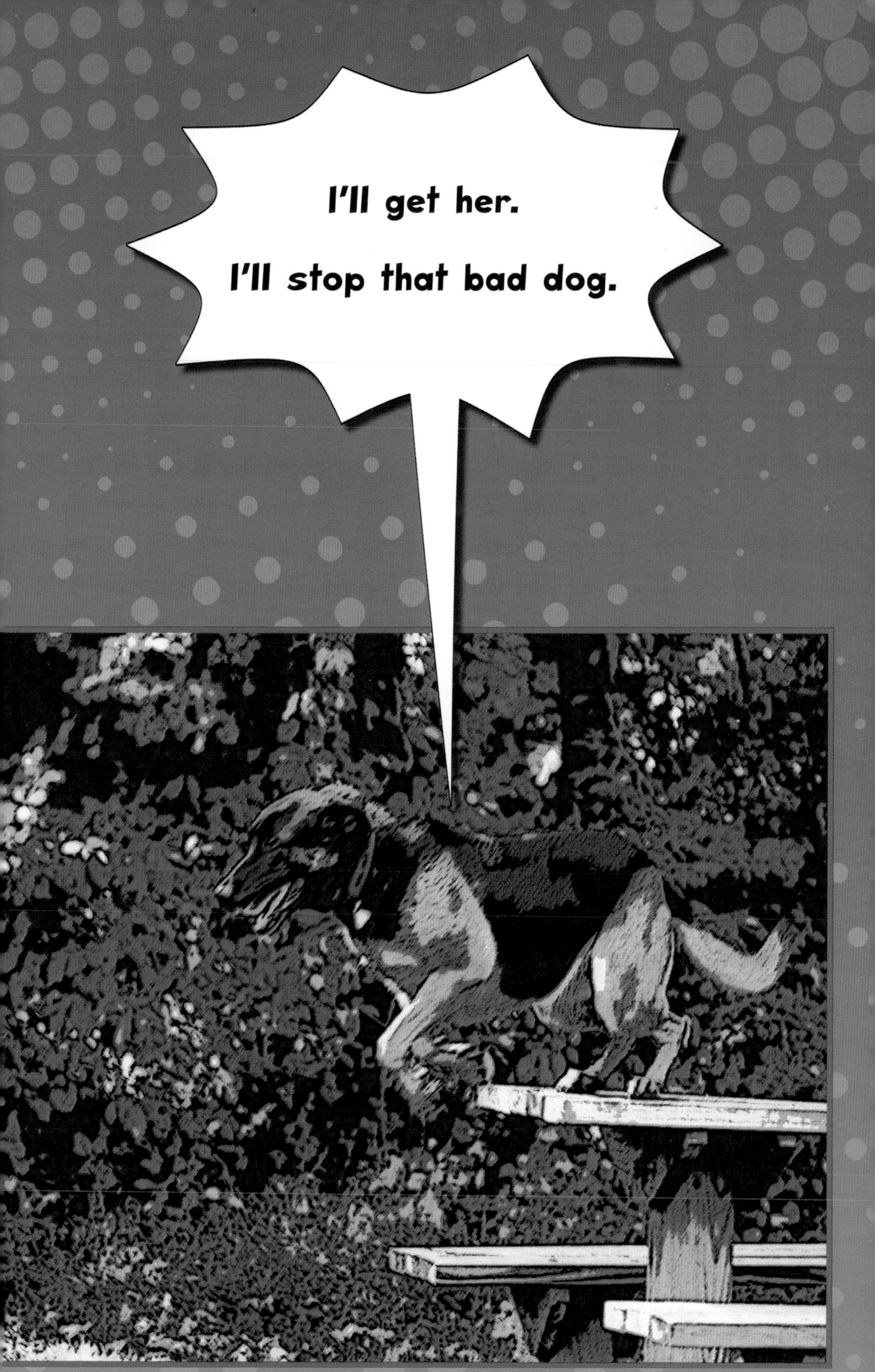
I'll get her.
I'll stop that bad dog.

I love hot dogs.

I do. I do.

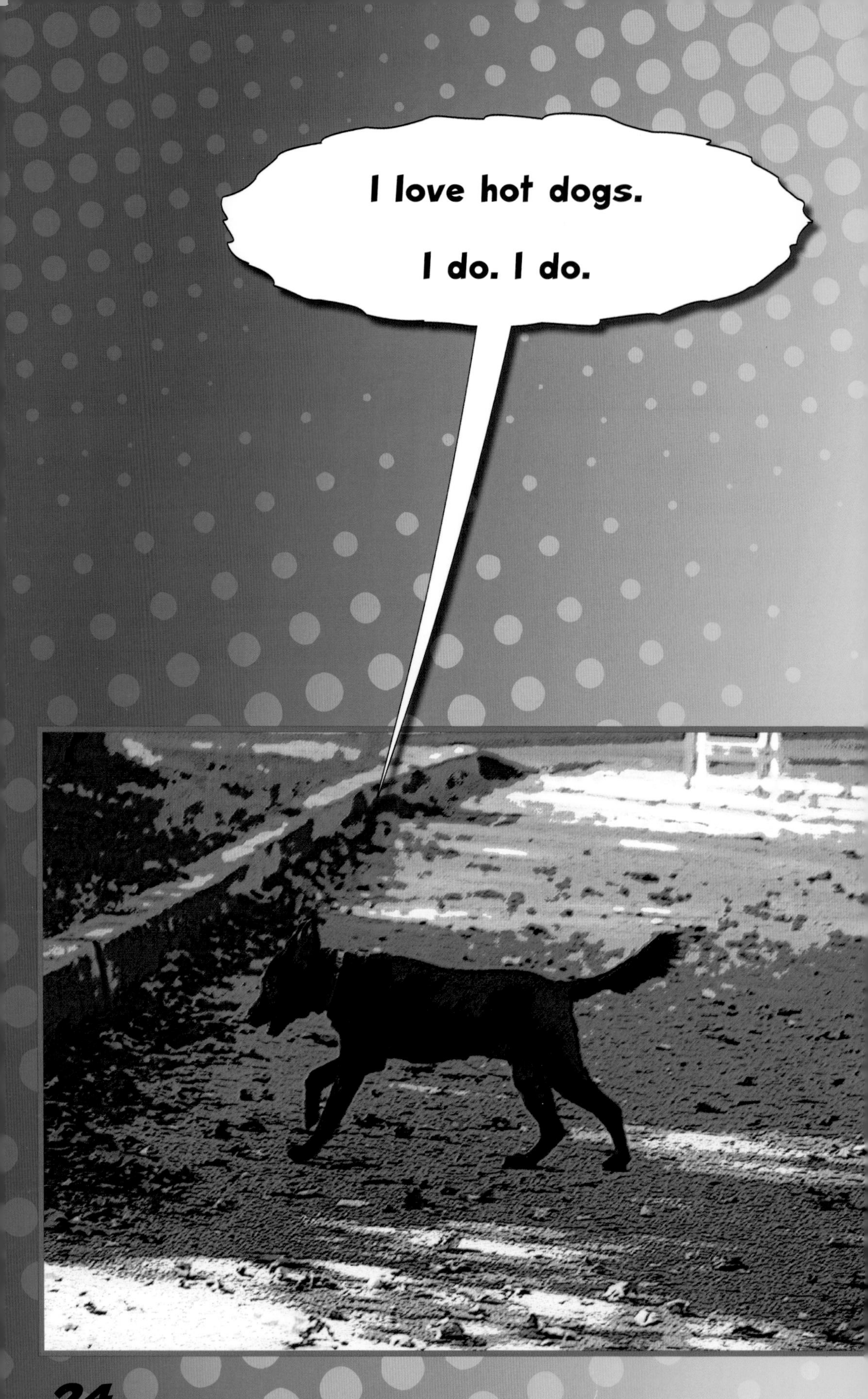

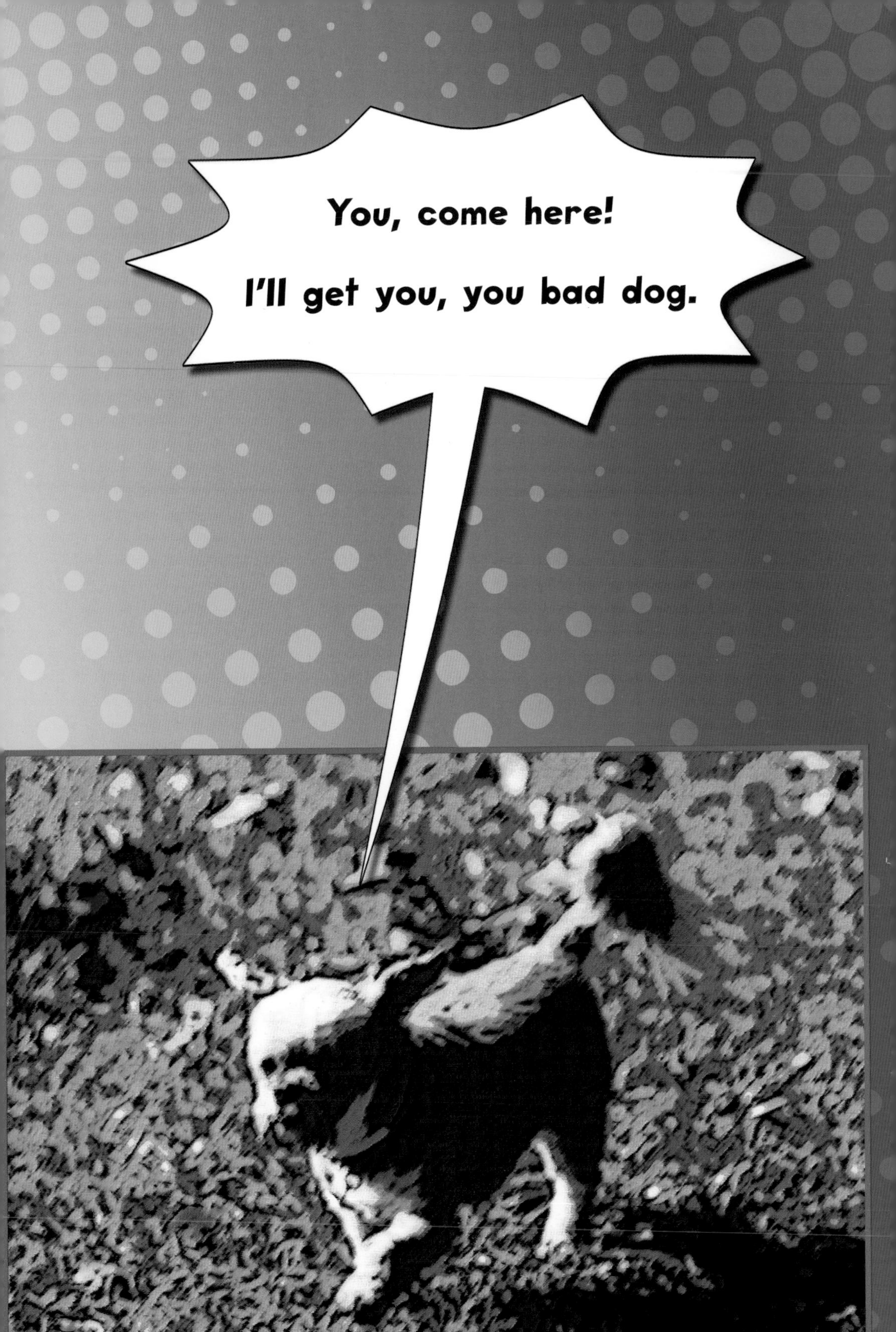
You, come here!
I'll get you, you bad dog.

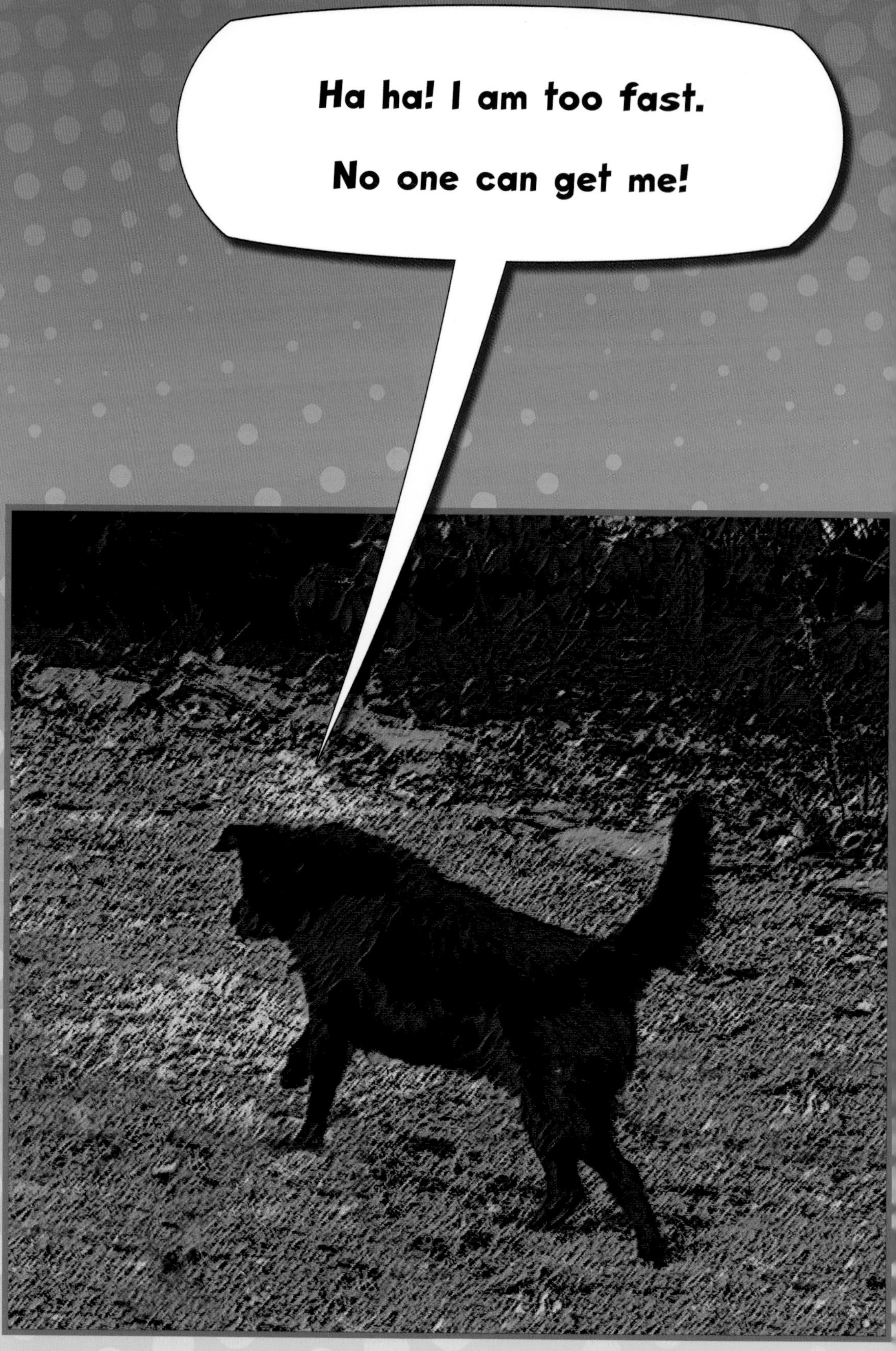
Ha ha! I am too fast.
No one can get me!

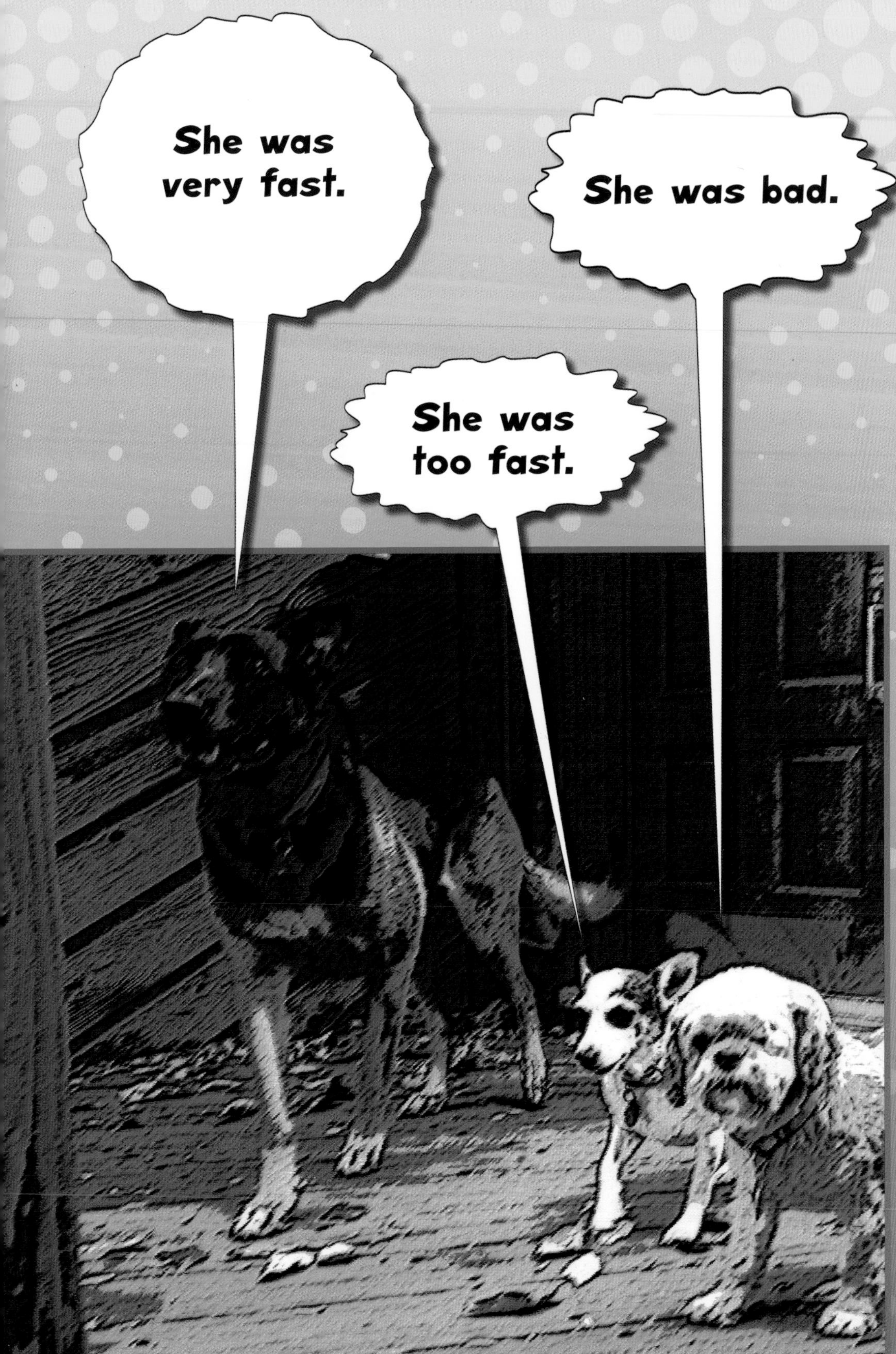
She was very fast.
She was bad.
She was too fast.

RESCUED

Juniper is a 14-year-old terrier mix who enjoys sneaking out of her yard, eating treats, visiting all the neighbors, going on very long walks, and playing tug-of-war.

RESCUED

Ladybug is a 10-year-old, one-eyed Shih-Tzu mix. She lost her eye when she was 6, but she manages fine without it. She loves eggs for breakfast and chicken treats at bedtime.

RESCUED

Viper is a 10-year-old Belgian Shepherd. She is very smart and can do lots of cool things like fetch the newspaper and play frisbee. She likes to get lots of exercise.

RESCUED

Annie is a 14-year-old Rat Terrier. She loves running through the woods with Viper. When she was younger, she enjoyed riding on a motorcycle. Now, she likes riding in the car.

WORD ATTACK STRATEGIES

STOP	**Stop** if something doesn't look right, sound right, or make sense.
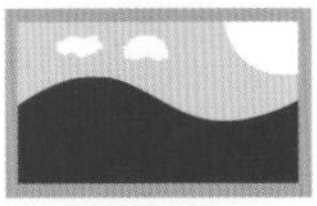	Look at the **picture**.
s____	Say the **first letter** sound.
sm____	**Blend:** Say the first two letters.
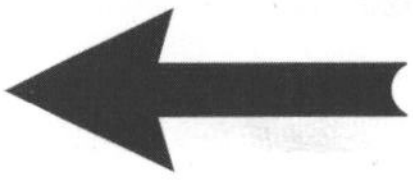	**Reread:** Go back and try again.
■ell	**Cover** part of the word.
sm(ell)	**Chunk**: Look for parts you know.
tell yell	Think of a word that looks the same and **rhymes**.
blank	Say **"blank,"** read on, and come back.
a e i o u	Try a **different sound** for the vowel.